The Diary of Adam and Eve

T0149173

The Diary
of Adam and Eve

and other Adamic Stories

Mark Twain

Published by Hesperus Press Limited
28 Mortimer Street, London W1W 7RD
www.hesperuspress.com

This collection first published by Hesperus Press Limited, 2002
This edition printed 2014

'Extract from Eve's Autobiography', 'Passage from Eve's Autobiography'
from *Letters from the Earth* by Mark Twain, edited by Bernard DeVoto
Copyright 1938, 1944, 1946, 1959, 1962 by The Mark Twain Company.
Copyright 1942 by The President and Fellows of Harvard College.
Reprinted by permission of HarperCollins Publishers Inc.

Foreword © John Updike, 2002

Designed and typeset by Fraser Muggeridge

ISBN: 978-1-84391-005-3

CONTENTS

FOREWORD

Most nineteenth-century Americans, even if not convention-
ally churchgoing, grew up with the sayings and stories of
the Bible. The Missourian Samuel Clemens, who became the
writer Mark Twain, was no exception; but where a literalist
interpretation of the Bible spelled comfort, if vaguely, to
most listeners, to Mark Twain it increasingly offered a pur-
chase on the absurdity of the Christian religion and the cruelty
of the Creator. Like the atheist evangel Robert Ingersoll, he
sharply turned the Bible against itself. To burlesque its myths
took merely a plain retelling in a down-to-earth American
voice. With Adam, the first human victim of God's whimsical
tyranny, Clemens enjoyed a natural identification: he saw his
own life in terms of lost paradises* – the lost paradise of the
Hannibal, Missouri, of his childhood, and later, of his family
life in Hartford, Connecticut, from 1875 to 1891, where he
wrote, among much else, his two masterpieces, *Huckleberry
Finn* and *Life on the Mississippi*. After 1891 he fell, as it were,
into a wilderness of business failure, bankruptcy, family illness,
celebrity, travel, loneliness, and increasingly dark views of God
and humankind.

His inspirations were ever wayward; no great writer more
haphazardly courted greatness. 'Extracts from Adam's Diary'
existed in some form before 1893, when Clemens received a
request for a humorous piece on Niagara Falls to be part of a
souvenir book for the 1893 World Fair in Buffalo, New York.
At first he declined, but then saw that 'Adam's Diary' might
be relocated to an Eden that contained Niagara Falls. This

---

* This insight, and much of the bibliographic information here, come from
A Reader's Guide to the Short Stories of Mark Twain, by James D. Wilson
(Boston: G.K. Hall & Co., 1987).

insouciant transposition served its purpose; *The Niagara Book* published his contribution, though the author only received five hundred dollars of the promised thousand. In 1905, a request came from *Harper's Magazine* for a contribution to their Christmas issue, and Clemens complied with a diary for Eve that led him to consider Adam's anew. Hoping for *Harper's* to publish the two diaries together, he cut seven hundred words from Adam's, and wrote some new pages in Adam's voice which he inserted, italicised, into 'Eve's Diary'. To the editor of *Harper's* he pronounced the result 'dam[n] good – sixty times as good as it was'. The magazine published only 'Eve's Diary', however, and the two were not published together, as they appear here, until 1931.

At least three posthumously published pieces – 'That Day in Eden', 'Eve Speaks', and 'Eve's Autobiography' – extend Mark Twain's animation of Adam and Eve; 'Eve Speaks', for instance, dated at around 1900, begins with her bewildered questioning of God and His angelic agents ('They drove us from the Garden with their swords of flame, the fierce cherubim. And what had we done? We meant no harm. We were ignorant, and did as any other children might do...'), proceeds to describe her pathetic misapprehension that her slain son Abel is merely sleeping, and ends with this brief entry from Satan's Diary:

'Death has entered the world, the creatures are perishing; one of The Family is fallen; the product of the Moral Sense is complete. The Family think ill of death – they will change their minds.'

As Mark Twain became, with the death of his favourite daughter, Suzie, increasingly isolated and lonely, he identified more and more with the first, singular man. He came to see himself as '*the* American' and even '*the* man'. His quarrel with God became more savage in the wake of his financial miseries and family tragedy, which eventually carried off another daughter, Jean. These Adamic diaries are one of the many modes with which, in the last decade of his life, Twain sought to confront ultimate questions and the great Christian fraud, in writings whose blasphemous and nihilistic nature by and large prevented publication: 'The Mysterious Stranger' and 'Letters from the Earth' are the most extensive, most vehement examples.

'The Diary of Adam and Eve' itself is a more agreeable work, toying with Genesis in a mood less of indignation than affection, taking the myth as a paradigm of the relations between the sexes. Adam is a typical male, into whose solitude a talkative, inquisitive, organising, long-haired creature has abruptly intruded. He is slow to recognise her as closer to him than to the other animals, and the revelation of her gender brings no accompaniment of desire: 'What she is were nothing to me if she would but go by herself and not talk.' She spoils his fun, whose main ingredient is going over Niagara Falls, in a barrel or without. When Eve produces children, he has no idea where they came from, and is very slow to see that they resemble, in miniature, him. Boyishly, he stands outside all social processes; he attempts to recover his pristine solitude outside of Eden, where she follows him and feeds him the forbidden apples. Eating them is against his principles, but he finds – in the voice of Mark Twain the immoralist – 'that principles have no real force except when one is well fed.'

Eve, on the other hand, is, in the feminist term of fashion, 'relational' to a fault. Like Adam, she takes her mate for a mere animal at first. She resents its interest in resting ('It would tire me to rest so much'), but when it speaks, she begins to fall in love: 'For I love to talk; I talk, all day, and in my sleep, too, and I am very interesting, but if I had another to talk to I could be twice as interesting, and would never stop, if desired.' Eve is embodied activity; she talks all day, gives things their names, discovers fire, befriends animals, and perpetrates a wifely love beyond all limit and reason. Her attempt to plumb her love for Adam reaches into female masochism, in this age when Freud and Havelock Ellis were anatomising Eros:

'Then why is it that I love him? *Merely because he is masculine*, I think.

At bottom he is good, and I love him for that, but I could love him without it. If he should beat me and abuse me, I should go on loving him. I know it, it is a matter of sex, I think.'

'Eve's Diary' makes a bold foray into female sexuality, a territory that Bernard DeVoto thought presented a conspicuous gap in Mark Twain's world: 'None of Mark Twain's nubile girls, young women, or young matrons are believable.' Yet Clemens, a product of the trafficked Mississippi and the Wild West, who did not marry until he was thirty-five, was no prude; in 'Letters from the Earth', he dared complain about the lack of copulation in heaven: 'From youth to middle age all men and women prize copulation above all other pleasures combined,' brief as its 'overwhelming climax' is, compared to the 'supremest ecstasies unbroken and without withdrawal for centuries' that angels purportedly enjoy. Eve's indiscriminate subjection to the masculine principle has something in it of Victorian hysteria and something of biological truth, the hot truth. Twain is at his hottest, his least guarded, in these sweeping avowals of Eve's. Her diary concludes with Adam's saying at her grave that 'wheresoever she was, there was Eden': a lightly disguised tribute to Clemens' recently deceased wife, Olivia. Adam and Eve, half-mocked, yet gave him a path into intimate feelings unapproached by the beguiling, brusquely fantastic, altogether masculine yarns that dominate his *oeuvre*.

– John Updike, 2002

The Diary
of Adam and Eve

PART I

EXTRACTS FROM ADAM'S DIARY

MONDAY

This new creature with the long hair is a good deal in the way. It is always hanging around and following me about. I don't like this; I am not used to company. I wish it would stay with the other animals... Cloudy today, wind in the east; think we shall have rain. ... *We?* Where did I get that word? I remember now – the new creature used it.

TUESDAY

Been examining the great waterfall. It is the finest thing on the estate, I think. The new creature calls it Niagara Falls – why, I am sure I do not know. Says it *looks* like Niagara Falls. That is not a reason; it is mere waywardness and imbecility. I get no chance to name anything myself. The new creature names everything that comes along, before I can get in a protest. And always that same pretext is offered – it *looks* like the thing. There is the dodo, for instance. Says the moment one looks at it one sees at a glance that it 'looks like a dodo'. It will have to keep that name, no doubt. It wearies me to fret about it, and it does no good, anyway. Dodo! It looks no more like a dodo than I do.

WEDNESDAY

Built me a shelter against the rain, but could not have it to myself in peace. The new creature intruded. When I tried to put it out it shed water out of the holes it looks with, and wiped it away with the back of its paws, and made a noise such as some of the other animals make when they are in distress. I wish it would not talk; it is always talking. That sounds like a cheap fling at the poor creature, a slur; but I do not mean it so. I have never heard the human voice before, and any new and strange sound intruding itself here upon the solemn hush of these dreaming solitudes offends my ear and seems a false note. And this new sound is so close to me; it is right at my shoulder, right at my ear, first on one side and then on the other, and I am used only to sounds that are more or less distant from me.

FRIDAY

The naming goes recklessly on, in spite of anything I can do. I had a very good name for the estate, and it was musical and pretty – Garden of Eden. Privately, I continue to call it that, but not any longer publicly. The new creature says it is all woods and rocks and scenery, and therefore has no resemblance to a garden. Says it *looks* like a park, and does not look like anything *but* a park. Consequently, without consulting me, it has been new-named Niagara Falls Park. This is sufficiently high-handed, it seems to me. And already there is a sign up:

KEEP OFF THE GRASS

My life is not as happy as it was.

SATURDAY

The new creature eats too much fruit. We are going to run short, most likely. 'We' again – that is *its* word; mine, too, now, from hearing it so much. Good deal of fog this morning. I do not go out in the fog myself. The new creature does. It goes out in all weathers, and stumps right in with its muddy feet. And talks. It used to be so pleasant and quiet here.

SUNDAY

Pulled through. This day is getting to be more and more trying. It was selected and set apart last November as a day of rest. I had already six of them per week before. This morning

6

found the new creature trying to clod apples out of that forbidden tree.

MONDAY

The new creature says its name is Eve. That is all right, I have no objections. I said it was superfluous then. The word evidently raised me in its respect; and indeed it is a large, good word and will bear repetition. It says it is not an *it*, it is a *she*. This is probably doubtful; yet it is all one to me. What she is were nothing to me if she would but go by herself and not talk.

TUESDAY

She has littered the whole estate with execrable names and offensive signs:

THIS WAY TO THE WHIRLPOOL
THIS WAY TO GOAT ISLAND
CAVE OF THE WINDS THIS WAY

She says this park would make a tidy summer resort if there were any custom for it. Summer resort – another invention of hers – just words, without any meaning. What is a summer resort? But it is best not to ask her; she has such a rage for explaining.

FRIDAY

She has taken to beseeching me to stop going over the Falls. What harm does it do? Says it makes her shudder. I wonder why; I have always done it – always liked the plunge and coolness. I supposed it was what the Falls were for. They have no other use that I can see, and they must have been made for something. She says they were only made for scenery – like the rhinoceros and the mastodon.

I went over the Falls in a barrel – not satisfactory to her. Went over in a tub – still not satisfactory. Swam the Whirlpool and the Rapids in a fig-leaf suit. It got much damaged. Hence, tedious complaints about my extravagance. I am too much hampered here. What I need is change of scene.

SATURDAY

I escaped last Tuesday night, and travelled two days, and built me another shelter in a secluded place, and obliterated my tracks as well as I could. But she hunted me out by means of a beast which she has tamed and calls a wolf, and came making that pitiful noise again, and shedding that water out of the places she looks with. I was obliged to return with her, but will presently emigrate again when occasion offers. She engages herself in many foolish things – among others, to study out why the animals called lions and tigers live on grass and flowers, when, as she says, the sort of teeth they wear would indicate that they were intended to eat each other. This is foolish, because to do that would be to kill each other, and that would introduce what, as I understand it, is called 'death', and death, as I have been told, has not yet entered the Park. Which is a pity, on some accounts.

SUNDAY

Pulled through.

MONDAY

I believe I see what the week is for: it is to give time to rest up from the weariness of Sunday. It seems a good idea... She has been climbing that tree again. Clodded her out of it. She said nobody was looking. Seems to consider that a sufficient justification for chancing any dangerous thing. Told her that. The word justification moved her admiration – and envy, too, I thought. It is a good word.

TUESDAY

She told me she was made out of a rib taken from my body. This is at least doubtful, if not more than that. I have not missed any rib… She is in much trouble about the buzzard: says grass does not agree with it, is afraid she can't raise it; thinks it was intended to live on decayed flesh. The buzzard must get along the best it can with what it is provided. We cannot overturn the whole scheme to accommodate the buzzard.

SATURDAY

She fell in the pond yesterday when she was looking at herself in it, which she is always doing. She nearly strangled, and said it was most uncomfortable. This made her sorry for the creatures which live in there, which she calls fish, for she continues to fasten names onto things that don't need them and don't come when they are called by them, which is a matter of no consequence to her. She is such a numskull, anyway… So she got a lot of them out and brought them in last night, and put them in my bed to keep warm, but I have noticed them now and then all day, and I don't see that they are any happier there than they were before, only quieter. When night comes I shall throw them outdoors. I will not sleep with them again, for I find them clammy and unpleasant to lie among when a person hasn't anything on.

SUNDAY

Pulled through.

TUESDAY

She has taken up with a snake now. The other animals are glad, for she was always experimenting with them and bothering them; and I am glad because the snake talks, and this enables me to get a rest.

FRIDAY

She says the snake advises her to try the fruit of that tree, and says the result will be a great and fine and noble education. I told her there would be another result, too – it would introduce death into the world. That was a mistake. It had been better to keep the remark to myself; it only gave her an idea – she could save the sick buzzard, and furnish fresh meat to the despondent lions and tigers. I advised her to keep away from the tree. She said she wouldn't. I foresee trouble. Will emigrate.

WEDNESDAY

I have had a variegated time. I escaped last night, and rode a horse all night as fast as he could go, hoping to get clear out of the Park and hide in some other country before the trouble should begin; but it was not to be. About an hour after sun-up, as I was riding through a flowery plain where thousands of animals were grazing, slumbering, or playing with each other, according to their wont, all of a sudden they broke into a tempest of frightful noises, and in one moment the plain was a frantic commotion and every beast was destroying its neighbour. I knew what it meant – Eve had eaten that fruit, and death was come into the world… The tigers ate my horse, paying no attention when I ordered them to desist, and they would have eaten me if I had stayed – which I didn't, but went away in much haste…

I found this place, outside the Park, and was fairly comfortable for a few days, but she has found me out. Found me out, and has named the place Tonawanda – says it *looks* like that. In fact I was not sorry she came, for there are but meagre pickings here, and she brought some of those apples. I was obliged to eat them, I was so hungry. It was against my principles, but I find that principles have no real force except when one is well fed…

She came curtained in boughs and bunches of leaves, and when I asked her what she meant by such nonsense, and snatched them away and threw them down, she tittered and blushed. I had never seen a person titter and blush before, and to me it seemed unbecoming and idiotic. She said I would soon know how it was myself. This was correct. Hungry as I was, I laid down the apple half-eaten – certainly the best one I ever saw, considering the lateness of the season – and arrayed myself in the discarded boughs and branches, and then spoke to her with some severity and ordered her to go and get some more and not make such a spectacle of herself. She did it, and after this we crept down to where the wild-beast battle had been, and collected some skins, and I made her patch together a couple of suits proper for public occasions. They are uncomfortable, it is true, but stylish, and that is the main point about clothes… I find she is a good deal of a companion. I see I should be lonesome and depressed without her, now that I have lost my property. Another thing, she says it is ordered that we work for our living hereafter. She will be useful. I will superintend.

TEN DAYS LATER
She accuses *me* of being the cause of our disaster! She says, with apparent sincerity and truth, that the serpent assured her

11

that the forbidden fruit was not apples, it was chestnuts. I said I was innocent, then, for I had not eaten any chestnuts. She said the serpent informed her that 'chestnut' was a figurative term, meaning an aged and mouldy joke. I turned pale at that, for I have made many jokes to pass the weary time, and some of them could have been of that sort, though I had honestly supposed that they were new when I made them. She asked me if I had made one just at the time of the catastrophe. I was obliged to admit that I had made one to myself, though not aloud. It was this: I was thinking about the Falls, and I said to myself, 'How wonderful it is to see that vast body of water tumble down there!' Then in an instant a bright thought flashed into my head, and I let it fly, saying, 'It would be a deal more wonderful to see it tumble *up* there!' – and I was just about to kill myself with laughing at it when all nature broke loose in war and death, and I had to flee for my life. 'There,' she said with triumph, 'that is just it. The Serpent mentioned that very jest, and called it the First Chestnut, and said it was coeval with the creation.' Alas, I am indeed to blame. Would that I were not witty. Oh, that I had never had that radiant thought!

NEXT YEAR

We have named it Cain. She caught it while I was up-country trapping on the north shore of the Eerie; caught it in the timber a couple of miles from our dugout – or it might have been four, she isn't certain which. It resembles us in some ways, and may be a relation. That is what she thinks, but this is an error, in my judgement. The difference in size warrants the conclusion that it is a different and new kind of animal – a fish, perhaps, though when I put it in the water to see, it sank, and she plunged in and snatched it out before there was opportunity for the experiment to determine the matter. I still think it is a fish, but she is indifferent about what it is, and will not let me have it to try. I do not understand this. The coming of the creature seems to have changed her whole nature and made her unreasonable about experiments. She thinks more of it than she does of any of the other animals, but is not able to explain why. Her mind is disordered – everything shows it. Sometimes she carries the fish in her arms half the night when it complains and wants to get to the water. At such times the water comes out of the places in her face that she looks out of, and she pats the fish on the back and makes soft sounds with her mouth to soothe it, and betrays sorrow and solicitude in a hundred ways. I have never seen her act like this with any other fish, and it troubles me greatly. She used to carry the young tigers around so, and play with them, before we lost our property, but it was only play. She never took on about them like this when their dinner disagreed with them.

SUNDAY

She doesn't work Sundays, but lies around all tired out, and likes to have the fish wallow over her, and she makes fool noises to amuse it, and pretends to chew its paws, and that makes it laugh. I have not seen a fish before that could laugh. This makes me doubt… I have come to like Sunday myself. Superintending all the week tires a body so. There ought to be more Sundays. In the old days they were tough, but now they come handy.

WEDNESDAY

It isn't a fish. I cannot quite make out what it is. It makes curious devilish noises when not satisfied, and says 'goo-goo' when it is. It is not one of us for it doesn't walk; it is not a bird for it doesn't fly; it is not a frog for it doesn't hop; it is not a snake for it doesn't crawl. I feel sure it is not a fish, though I cannot get a chance to find out whether it can swim or not. It merely lies around, and mostly on its back, with its feet up. I have not seen any other animal do that before. I said I believed it was an enigma; but she only admired the word without understanding it. In my judgement it is either an enigma or some kind of a bug. If it dies, I will take it apart and see what its arrangements are. I never had a thing perplex me so.

THREE MONTHS LATER

The perplexity augments instead of diminishing. I sleep but little. It has ceased from lying around, and goes about on its four legs now. Yet it differs from the other four-legged animals, in that its front legs are unusually short. Consequently this causes the main part of its person to stick up uncomfortably high in the air, and this is not attractive. It is built much as we are, but its method of travelling shows that it is not of our breed. The short front legs and long hind ones indicate that it is of the kangaroo family, but it is a marked variation of the species, since the true kangaroo hops, whereas this one never does. Still it is a curious and interesting variety, and has not been catalogued before. As I discovered it, I have felt justified in securing the credit of the discovery by attaching my name to it, and hence have called it *Kangaroorum Adamiensis*…. It must have been a young one when it came, for it has grown exceedingly since. It must be five times as big, now, as it was then, and when discontented it is able to make from twenty-two to thirty-eight times the noise it made at first. Coercion does not modify this, but has the contrary effect. For this reason I discontinued the system. She reconciles it by persuasion, and by giving it things which she had and she had

14

previously told me she wouldn't give it. As already observed, I was not at home when it first came, and she told me she found it in the woods. It seems odd that it should be the only one, yet it must be so, for I have worn myself out these many weeks trying to find another one to add to my collection, and for this one to play with – for surely then it would be quieter and we could tame it more easily. But I find none, nor any vestige of any, and strangest of all, no tracks. It has to live on the ground, it cannot help itself; therefore, how does it get about without leaving a track? I have set a dozen traps, but they do no good. I catch all small animals except that one; animals that merely go into the trap out of curiosity, I think, to see what the milk is there for. They never drink it.

THREE MONTHS LATER

The kangaroo still continues to grow, which is very strange and perplexing. I never knew one to be so long getting its growth. It has fur on its head now; not like kangaroo fur, but exactly like our hair except that it is much finer and softer, and instead of being black is red. I am like to lose my mind over the capricious and harassing developments of this unclassifiable zoological freak. If I could catch another one – but that is hopeless. It is a new variety, and the only sample; this is plain. But I caught a true kangaroo and brought it in, thinking that this one, being lonesome, would rather have that for company than have no kin at all, or any animal it could feel a nearness to or get sympathy from in its forlorn condition here among strangers who do not know its ways or habits, or what to do to make it feel that it is among friends. But it was a mistake – it went into such fits at the sight of the kangaroo that I was convinced it had never seen one before. I pity the poor noisy little animal, but there is nothing I can do to make it happy. If I could tame it... But that is out of the question; the more I try the worse I seem to make it. It grieves me to the heart to see it in its little storms of sorrow and passion. I wanted to let it go, but she wouldn't hear of it. That seemed cruel and not like her; and yet she may be right. It might be lonelier than ever, for since I cannot find another one, how could *it*?

FIVE MONTHS LATER

It is not a kangaroo. No, for it supports itself by holding to her finger, and thus goes a few steps on its hind legs, and then falls down. It is probably some kind of a bear; and yet it has no tail – as yet – and no fur, except on its head. It still keeps on growing – that is a curious circumstance, for bears get their growth earlier than this. Bears are dangerous – since our catastrophe – and I shall not be satisfied to have this one prowling about the place much longer without a muzzle on. I have offered to get her a kangaroo if she would let this one go, but it did no good. She is determined to run us into all sort of foolish risks, I think. She was not like this before she lost her mind.

A FORTNIGHT LATER

I examined its mouth. There is no danger yet: it has only one tooth. It has no tail yet. It makes more noise now than it ever did before – and mainly at night. I have moved out. But I shall go over, mornings, to breakfast, and see if it has more teeth. If it gets a mouthful of teeth it will be time for it to go, tail or no tail, for a bear does not need a tail in order to be dangerous.

FOUR MONTHS LATER

I have been off hunting and fishing a month, up in the region that she calls Buffalo; I don't know why, unless it is because there are not any buffaloes there. Meantime the bear has learned to paddle around all by itself on its hind legs, and says 'poppa' and 'momma'. It is certainly a new species. This resemblance to words may be purely accidental, of course, and may have no purpose or meaning; but even in that case it is still extraordinary, and is a thing which no other bear can do. This imitation of speech, taken together with general absence of fur and entire absence of tail, sufficiently indicates that this is a new kind of bear. The further study of it will be exceedingly interesting. Meantime I will go off on a far expedition among the forests of the north and make an exhaustive search. There must certainly be another one somewhere, and this one will be less dangerous when it has company of its own species. I will go straightaway, but I will muzzle this one first.

THREE MONTHS LATER

It has been a weary, weary hunt, yet I have had no success. In the meantime, without stirring from the home estate, she has caught another one! I never saw such luck. I might have hunted these woods a hundred years, I would never have run across that thing.

NEXT DAY

I have been comparing the new one with the old one, and it is perfectly plain that they are the same breed. I was going to stuff one of them for my collection, but she is prejudiced against it for some reason or other, so I have relinquished the idea, though I think it is a mistake. It would be an irreparable loss to science if they should get away. The old one is tamer than it was and can laugh and talk like the parrot, having learned this, no doubt, from being with the parrot so much, and having the imitative faculty in a highly developed degree. I shall be astonished if it turns out to be a new kind of parrot; and yet I ought not to be astonished, for it has already been everything else it could think of since those first days when it was a fish. The new one is as ugly now as the old one was at first; has the same sulphur-and-raw-meat complexion and the same singular head without any fur on it. She calls it Abel.

TEN YEARS LATER

They are *boys*; we found it out long ago. It was their coming in that small, immature shape that puzzled us; we were not used to it. There are some girls now. Abel is a good boy, but if Cain had stayed a bear it would have improved him. After all these years, I see that I was mistaken about Eve in the beginning; it is better to live outside the Garden with her than inside without her. At first I thought she talked too much; but now I should be sorry to have that voice fall silent and pass out of my life. Blessed be the chestnut that brought us near together and taught me to know the goodness of her heart and the sweetness of her spirit!

PART II

EVE'S DIARY

Translated from the original

I am almost a whole day old now. I arrived yesterday. That is as it seems to me. And it must be so, for if there was a day-before-yesterday, I was not there when it happened, or I should remember it. It could be, of course, that it did happen, and that I was not noticing. Very well; I will be watchful now, and if any day-before-yesterdays happen I will make a note of it. It will be best to start right and not let the record get confused, for some instinct tells me that these details are going to be important to the historian some day. For I feel like an experiment, I feel exactly like an experiment; it would be impossible for a person to feel more like an experiment than I do, and so I am coming to feel convinced that that is what I *am* – an experiment; just an experiment, and nothing more.

Then if I am an experiment, am I the whole of it? No, I think not. I think the rest of it is part of it. I am the main part of it, but I think the rest of it has its share in the matter. Is my position assured, or do I have to watch it and take care of it? The latter, perhaps. Some instinct tells me that eternal vigilance is the price of supremacy. (That is a good phrase, I think, for one so young.)

Everything looks better today than it did yesterday. In the rush of finishing up yesterday, the mountains were left in a ragged condition, and some of the plains were so cluttered with rubbish and remnants that the aspects were quite distressing. Noble and beautiful works of arts should not be subjected to haste; and this majestic new world is indeed a most noble and beautiful work. And certainly marvellously near to being perfect, notwithstanding the shortness of the time. There are too many stars in some places and not enough in others, but that can be remedied presently, no doubt. The moon got loose last night, and slid down and fell out of the scheme – a very great loss. It breaks my heart to think of it.

There isn't another thing among the ornaments and decorations that is comparable to it for beauty and finish. It should have been fastened better. If we can only get it back again...

But of course there is no telling where it went to. And besides, whoever gets it will hide it. I know because I would do it myself. I believe I can be honest in all other matters, but I already begin to realise that the core and centre of my nature is love of the beautiful, a passion for the beautiful, and that it would not be safe to trust me with a moon that belonged to another person and that person didn't know I had it. I could give up a moon that I found in the daytime, because I should be afraid someone was looking; but if I found it in the dark, I am sure I should find some kind of an excuse for not saying anything about it. For I do love moons, they are so pretty and so romantic. I wish we had five or six. I would never go to bed. I should never get tired lying on the moss-bank and looking up at them.

Stars are good, too. I wish I could get some to put in my hair. But I suppose I never can. You would be surprised to find how far off they are, for they do not look it. When they first showed, last night, I tried to knock some down with a pole, but it didn't reach, which astonished me; then I tried clods till I was all tired out, but I never got one. It was because I am left-handed and cannot throw well. Even when I aimed at the one I wasn't after, I couldn't hit the other one, though I did make some close shots, for I saw the black blot of the clod sail right into the midst of the golden clusters forty or fifty times, just barely missing them, and if I could have held out a little longer maybe I could have got one.

So I cried a little, which was natural, I suppose, for one of my age, and after I was rested I got a basket and started for a place on the extreme rim of the circle, where the stars were close to the ground and I could get them with my hands, which would be better, anyway, because I could gather them tenderly then, and not break them. But it was further than I thought, and at last I had to give it up. I was so tired I couldn't drag my feet another step, and besides, they were sore and hurt me very much.

I couldn't get back home. It was too far and turning cold, but I found some tigers and nestled in among them and was most adorably comfortable, and their breath was sweet and pleasant, because they live on strawberries. I had never seen a tiger before, but I knew them in a minute by the stripes. If I could have one of those skins, it would make a lovely gown.

Today I am getting better ideas about distances. I was so eager to get hold of every pretty thing that I giddily grabbed for it, sometimes when it was too far off, and sometimes when it was six inches away but seemed a foot – alas, with thorns between! I learned a lesson; also I made an axiom, all out of my own head – my very first one: *The scratched Experiment shuns the thorn.* I think it is a very good one for one so young.

I followed the other Experiment around yesterday afternoon, at a distance, to see what it might be for, if I could. But I was not able to make out. I think it is a man. I had never seen a man, but it looked like one, and I feel sure that that is what it is. I realise that I feel more curiosity about it than about any of the other reptiles. If it is a reptile, and I suppose it is, for it has frowzy hair and blue eyes, and looks like a reptile. It has no hips – it tapers like a carrot, and when it stands, it spreads itself apart like a derrick, so I think it is a reptile, though it may be architecture.

I was afraid of it at first, and started to run every time it turned around, for I thought it was going to chase me; but by and by I found it was only trying to get away, so after that I was not timid anymore, but tracked it along, several hours, about twenty yards behind, which made it nervous and unhappy. At last it was a good deal worried, and climbed a tree. I waited a good while, then gave it up and went home.

Today the same thing over. I've got it up the tree again.

SUNDAY

It is up there yet. Resting, apparently. But that is a subterfuge: Sunday isn't the day of rest; Saturday is appointed for that. It looks to me like a creature that is more interested in resting than in anything else. It would tire me to rest so much. It tires me just to sit around and watch the tree. I do wonder what it is for; I never see it do anything.

They returned the moon last night, and I was *so* happy! I think it is very honest of them. It slid down and fell off again, but I was not distressed. There is no need to worry when one has those kind of neighbours; they will fetch it back. I wish I could do something to show my appreciation. I would like to send them some stars, for we have more than we can use. I mean I, not we, for I can see that the reptile cares nothing for such things.

It has low tastes, and is not kind. When I went there yesterday evening in the gloaming, it had crept down and was trying to catch the little speckled fishes that play in the pool, and I had to clod it to make it go up the tree again and let them alone. I wonder if *that* is what it is for? Hasn't it any heart? Hasn't it any compassion for those little creatures? Can it be that it was designed and manufactured for such ungentle work? It has the look of it. One of the clods took it back of the ear, and it used language. It gave me a thrill, for it was the first time I had ever heard speech, except my own. I did not understand the words, but they seemed expressive.

24

When I found it could talk I felt a new interest in it, for I love to talk; I talk all day, and in my sleep, too, and I am very interesting, but if I had another to talk to I could be twice as interesting, and would never stop, if desired.

If this reptile is a man, it isn't an *it*, is it? That wouldn't be grammatical, would it? I think it would be *he*. I think so. In that case one would parse it thus: nominative, *he*; dative, *him*; positive, *his'n*. Well, I will consider it a man and call it he until it turns out to be something else. This will be handier than having so many uncertainties.

NEXT WEEK SUNDAY

All the week I tagged around after him and tried to get acquainted. I had to do the talking, because he was shy, but I didn't mind it. He seemed pleased to have me around, and I used the sociable 'we' a good deal, because it seemed to flatter him to be included.

WEDNESDAY

We are getting along very well indeed, now, and getting better and better acquainted. He does not try to avoid me anymore, which is a good sign, and shows that he likes to have me with him. That pleased me, and I study to be useful to him in every way I can, so as to increase his regard. During the last day or two I have taken all the work of naming things off his hands, and this has been a great relief to him, for he has not gift in that line, and is evidently very grateful. He can't think of a rational name to save him, but I do not let him see that I am aware of his defect. Whenever a new creature comes along I name it before he has time to expose himself by an awkward silence. In this way I have saved him many embarrassments. I have no defect like his. The minute I set eyes on an animal I know what it is. I don't have to reflect a moment; the right name comes out instantly, just as if it were an inspiration, as no doubt it is, for I am sure it wasn't in me half a minute before. I seem to know just by the shape of the creature and the way it acts what animal it is.

When the dodo came along he thought it was a wildcat – I saw it in his eye. But I saved him. And I was careful not to do it in a way that could hurt his pride. I just spoke up in a quite natural way of pleased surprise, and not as if I was dreaming of conveying information, and said, 'Well, I do declare, if there isn't the dodo!' I explained – without seeming to be explaining – how I knew it for a dodo, and although I thought maybe he was a little piqued that I knew the creature when he didn't, it was quite evident that he admired me. That was very agreeable, and I thought of it more than once with gratification before I slept. How little a thing can make us happy when we feel that we have earned it!

THURSDAY

My first sorrow. Yesterday he avoided me and seemed to wish I would not talk to him. I could not believe it, and thought there was some mistake, for I loved to be with him, and I loved to hear him talk, and so how could it be that he could feel unkind toward me when I had not done anything? But at last it seemed true, so I went away and sat lonely in the place where I first saw him the morning that we were made and I did not know what he was and was indifferent about me. But now it was a mournful place, and every little thing spoke of him, and my heart was very sore. I did not know why very clearly, for it was a new feeling. I had not experienced it before, and it was all a mystery, and I could not make it out.

But when night came I could not bear the lonesomeness,

and went to the new shelter which he has built to ask him what I had done that was wrong and how I could mend it and get back his kindness again. But he put me out in the rain, and it was my first sorrow.

SUNDAY

It was pleasant again, now, and I am happy. But those were heavy days; I do not think of them when I can help it. I tried to get him some of those apples, but I cannot learn how to throw straight. I failed, but I think the good intention pleased him. They were forbidden, and he says I shall come to harm; but so I come to harm through pleasing him, why shall I care for that harm?

MONDAY

This morning I told him my name, hoping it would interest him. But he did not care for it. It is strange. If he should tell me his name, I would care. I think it would be pleasanter in my ears than any other sound.

He talks very little. Perhaps it is because he is not bright, and is sensitive about it and wishes to conceal it. It is such a pity that he should feel so, for brightness is nothing; it is in the heart that the values lie. I wish I could make him understand that a loving good heart is riches, and riches enough, and that without it intellect is poverty.

Although he talks so little, he has quite a considerable vocabulary. This morning he used a surprisingly good word. He evidently recognised, himself, that it was a good one, for he worked it in twice afterwards, casually. It was not good casual art, still it showed that he possesses a certain quality of perfection. Without a doubt that seed can be made to grow, if cultivated.

Where did he get that word? I do not think I have ever used it.

No, he took no interest in my name. I tried to hide my disappointment, but I suppose I did not succeed. I went away and sat on the moss-bank with my feet in the water. It is where I go when I hunger for companionship, someone to look at, someone to talk to. It is not enough – that lovely white body painted there in the pool – but it is something, and something is better than utter loneliness. It talks when I talk; it is sad when I am sad; it comforts me with its sympathy. It says, 'Do not be downhearted, you poor friendless girl. I will be your friend.' It *is* a good friend to me, and my only one; it is my sister.

That first time that she forsook me! Ah, I shall never forget that – never, never. My heart was lead in my body! I said, 'She was all I had, and now she is gone!' In my despair I said, 'Break, my heart; I cannot bear my life any more!' and hid my face in my hands, and there was no solace for me. And when I took them away, after a little, there she was again, white and shining and beautiful, and I sprang into her arms!

That was perfect happiness. I had known happiness before, but it was not like this, which was ecstasy. I never doubted her afterwards. Sometimes she stayed away – maybe an hour, maybe almost the whole day – but I waited and I did not doubt. I said, 'She is busy, or she is gone on a journey, but she will come.' And it was so: she always did. At night she would not come if it was dark, for she was a timid little thing; but if there was a moon she would come. I am not afraid of the dark, but she is younger than I am; she was born after I was. Many and many are the visits I have paid her; she is my comfort and my refuge when my life is hard – and it is mainly that.

TUESDAY

All the morning I was at work improving the estate; and I purposely kept away from him in the hope that he would get lonely and come. But he did not.

At noon I stopped for the day and took my recreation by flitting all about with the bees and the butterflies and revelling in the flowers, those beautiful creatures that catch the smile of God out of the sky and preserve it! I gathered them, and made them into wreaths and garlands and clothed myself in them while I ate my luncheon – apples, of course – then I sat in the shade and wished and waited. But he did not come.

But no matter. Nothing would have come of it, for he does not care for flowers. He calls them rubbish, and cannot tell one from another, and thinks it is superior to feel like that. He does not care for me, he does not care for flowers, he does not care for the painted sky at eventide – is there anything he does care for, except building shacks to coop himself up in from the good clean rain, and thumping the melons, and sampling the grapes, and fingering the fruit on the trees, to see how those properties are coming along?

I laid a dry stick on the ground and tried to bore a hole in it with another one, in order to carry out a scheme that I had, and soon I got an awful fright. A thin, transparent bluish film rose out of the hole, and I dropped everything and ran! I thought it was a spirit, and I was so frightened! But I looked back, and it was not coming, so I leaned against a rock and rested and panted, and let my limbs go on trembling until they got steady again, then I crept warily back, alert, watching, and ready to fly if there was occasion. And when I was come near, I parted the branches of a rose bush and peeped through – wishing the man was about, I was looking so cunning and pretty – but the sprite was gone. I went there, and there was a pinch of delicate pink dust in the hole. I put my finger in, to feel it, and said 'Ouch!' and took it out again. It was a cruel pain. I put my finger in my mouth, and, by standing first on one foot and then the other, and grunting, I presently eased my misery. Then I was full of interest, and began to examine.

I was curious to know what the pink dust was. Suddenly the name of it occurred to me, though I had never heard of it before. It was *fire!* I was as certain of it as a person could be of anything in the world. So without hesitation I named it that – fire.

I had created something that didn't exist before; I had added a new thing to the world's uncountable properties. I realised this, and was proud of my achievement, and was going to run and find him and tell him about it, thinking to raise myself in his esteem – but I reflected, and did not do it. No – he would not care for it. He would ask what it was good for, and what could I answer? For if it was not *good* for something, but only beautiful, merely beautiful…

So I sighed, and did not go. For it wasn't good for anything; it could not build a shack, it could not improve melons, it could not hurry a fruit crop. It was useless, it was a foolishness and a vanity; he would despise it and say cutting words. But to me it was not despicable. I said, 'Oh, you fire, I love you, you dainty pink creature, for you are beautiful – and that is enough!' and was going to gather it to my breast. But refrained. Then I made another maxim out of my own head, though it was so nearly like the first one that I was afraid it was only a plagiarism: '*The burnt Experiment shuns the fire.*'

I wrought again; and when I had made a good deal of fire-dust I emptied it into a handful of dry brown grass, intending to carry it home and keep it always and play with it, but the wind struck it and it sprayed up and spat out at me fiercely, and I dropped it and ran. When I looked back the blue spirit was towering up and stretching and rolling away like a cloud, and instantly I thought of the name of it – *smoke*! – though, upon my word, I had never heard of smoke before.

Soon, brilliant yellow and red flares shot up through the smoke, and I named them in an instant – *flames* – and I was right, too, though these were the very first flames that had ever been in the world. They climbed the trees, they flashed splendidly in and out of the vast and increasing volume of tumbling smoke, and I had to clap my hands and laugh and dance in my rapture, it was so new and strange and so wonderful and so beautiful!

He came running, and stopped and gazed, and said not a word for many minutes. Then he asked what it was. Ah, it was too bad that he should ask such a direct question. I had to answer it, of course, and I did. I said it was fire. If it annoyed him that I should know and he must ask, that was not my fault; I had no desire to annoy him. After a pause he asked: 'How did it come?'

Another direct question, and it also had to have a direct answer. 'I made it.'

The fire was travelling further and further off. He went to the edge of the burned place and stood looking down, and said, 'What are these?'

'Fire coals.'

He picked up one to examine it, but changed his mind and put it down again. Then he went away. *Nothing* interests him.

But I was interested. There were ashes, grey and soft and delicate and pretty – I knew what they were at once. And the embers; I knew the embers, too. I found my apples, and raked them out, and was glad, for I am very young and my appetite is active. But I was disappointed, they were all burst open and spoiled. Spoiled apparently, but it was not so – they were better than raw ones. Fire is beautiful; some day it will be useful, I think.

FRIDAY

I saw him again, for a moment, last Monday at nightfall, but only for a moment. I was hoping he would praise me for trying to improve the estate, for I had meant well and had worked hard. But he was not pleased, and turned away and left me. He was also displeased on another account: I tried once more to persuade him to stop going over the Falls. That was because the fire had revealed to me a new passion – quite new, and distinctly different from love, grief, and those others which I had already discovered – fear. And it is horrible! I wish I had never discovered it; it gives me dark moments, it spoils my happiness, it makes me shiver and tremble and shudder. But I could not persuade him, for he has not discovered fear yet, and so he could not understand me.

EXTRACT FROM ADAM'S DIARY

Perhaps I ought to remember that she is very young, a mere girl, and make allowances. She is all interest, eagerness, vivacity, the world is to her a charm, a wonder, a mystery, a joy. She can't speak for delight when she finds a new flower, she must pet it and caress it and talk to it, and pour out endearing names upon it. And she is colour-mad: brown rocks, yellow sand, grey moss, green foliage, blue sky; the pearl of the dawn, the purple shadows on the mountains, the golden islands floating in crimson seas at sunset, the pallid moon sailing through the shredded cloud-rack, the star-jewels glittering in the wastes of space – none of them is of any practical value, so far as I can see, but because they have colour and majesty, that is enough for her, and she loses her mind over them. If she could quiet down and keep still a couple of minutes at a time, it would be a reposeful spectacle. In that case I think I could enjoy looking at her; indeed I am sure I could, for I am coming to realise that she is a quite remarkably comely creature – lithe, slender, trim, rounded, shapely, nimble, graceful; and once when she was standing marble-white and sun-drenched on a boulder, with her young head tilted back and her hand shading her eyes, watching the flight of a bird in the sky, I recognised that she was beautiful.

MONDAY NOON
If there is anything on the planet that she is not interested in, it is not in my list. There are animals that I am indifferent to, but it is not so with her. She has no discrimination, she takes to all of them, she thinks they are all treasures, every new one is welcome.

When the mighty brontosaurus came striding into camp, she

33

regarded it as an acquisition. I considered it a calamity – that is a good sample of the lack of harmony that prevails in our views of things. She wanted to domesticate it, I wanted to make it a present of the homestead and move out. She believed it could be tamed by kind treatment and would be a good pet; I said a pet twenty-one feet high and eighty-four feet long would be no proper thing to have about the place, because, even with the best intentions and without meaning any harm, it could set down on the house and mash it, for anyone could see by the look of its eye that it was absent-minded.

Still, her heart was set upon having that monster, and she couldn't give it up. She thought we could start a dairy with it, and wanted me to help her milk it. But I wouldn't; it was too risky. The sex wasn't right, and we hadn't any ladder anyway. Then she wanted to ride it and look at the scenery. Thirty or forty feet of its tail was lying on the ground, like a fallen tree, and she thought she could climb it, but she was mistaken. When she got to the steep place it was too slick and down she came, and would have hurt herself but for me.

Was she satisfied now? No. Nothing ever satisfies her but demonstration; untested theories are not in her line, and she won't have them. It is the right spirit, I concede it; it attracts me; I feel the influence of it; if I were with her more I think I should take it up myself. Well, she had one theory remaining about this colossus: she thought that if we could tame him and make him friendly, we could stand him in the river and use him for a bridge. It turned out that he was already plenty tame enough – at least as far as she was concerned – so she tried her theory, but it failed. Every time she got him properly placed in the river and went ashore to cross over on him, he came out and followed her around like a pet mountain. Like the other animals. They all do that.

Tuesday, Wednesday, Thursday and today – all without seeing him. It is a long time to be alone; still, it is better to be alone than unwelcome.

I *had* to have company – I was made for it, I think – so I made friends with the animals. They are just charming, and they have the kindest disposition and the politest ways. They never look sour, they never let you feel that you are intruding, they smile at you and wag their tail, if they've got one, and they are always ready for a romp or an excursion or anything you want to propose. I think they are perfect gentlemen. All these days we have had such good times, and it hasn't been lonesome for me, ever. Lonesome! No, I should say not. Why, there's always a swarm of them around – sometimes as much as four or five acres – you can't count them. And when you stand on a rock in the midst and look out over the furry expanse, it is so mottled and splashed and gay with colour and frisking sheen and sun-flash, and so rippled with stripes, that you might think it was a lake, only you know it isn't; and there's storms of sociable birds, and hurricanes of whirring wings; and when the sun strikes all that feathery commotion, you have a blazing up of all the colours you can think of, enough to put your eyes out.

We have made long excursions, and I have seen a great deal of the world – almost all of it, I think – and so I am the first traveller, and the only one. When we are on the march, it is an imposing sight – there's nothing like it anywhere. For comfort I ride a tiger or a leopard, because it is soft and has a round back that fits me, and because they are such pretty animals; but for long distances or for scenery I ride the elephant. He hoists me up with his trunk, but I can get off myself – when we are ready to camp, he sits and I slide down the back way.

The birds and animals are all friendly to each other, and

there are no disputes about anything. They all talk, and they all talk to me, but it must be a foreign language, for I cannot make out a word they say; yet they often understand me when I talk back, particularly the dog and the elephant. It makes me ashamed. It shows that they are brighter than I am, and are therefore my superiors. It annoys me, for I want to be the principal Experiment myself – and I intend to be, too.

I have learned a number of things, and am educated, now, but I wasn't at first. I was ignorant at first. At first it used to vex me that, with all my watching, I was never smart enough to be around when the water was running uphill; but now I do not mind it. I have experimented and experimented until now I know it never does run uphill, except in the dark. I know it does in the dark, because the pool never goes dry, which it would, of course, if the water didn't come back in the night. It is best to prove things by actual experiment, then you *know*, whereas if you depend on guessing and supposing and conjecturing, you will never get educated.

Some things you *can't* find out; but you will never know you can't by guessing and supposing: No, you have to be patient and go on experimenting until you find out that you can't find out. And it is delightful to have it that way – it makes the world so interesting. If there wasn't anything to find out, it would be dull. Even trying to find out and not finding out is just as interesting as trying to find out and finding out, and I don't know but more so. The secret of the water was a treasure until I *got* it; then the excitement all went away, and I recognised a sense of loss.

By experiment I know that wood swims, and dry leaves, and feathers, and plenty of other things; therefore by all that cumulative evidence you know that a rock will swim. But you have to put up with simply knowing it, for there isn't any way to prove it – up to now. But I shall find a way – then *that* excitement will go. Such things make me sad; because by and by when I have found out everything there won't be any more excitements, and I do love excitements so! The other night I couldn't sleep for thinking about it.

At first I couldn't make out what I was made for, but now I think it was to search out the secrets of this wonderful world and be happy and thank the Giver of it all for devising it. I think there are many things to learn yet – I hope so; and by economising and not hurrying too fast I think they will last weeks and weeks. I hope so. When you cast up a feather it sails away on the air and goes out of sight; then you throw up a clod and it doesn't. It comes down, every time. I have tried it and tried it, and it is always so. I wonder why it is? Of course it doesn't come down, but why should it *seem* to? I suppose it is an optical illusion. I mean, one of them is. I don't know which one. It may be the feather, it may be the clod; I can't prove which it is. I can only demonstrate that one or the other is a fake, and let a person take his choice.

By watching, I know that the stars are not going to last. I have seen some of the best ones melt and run down the sky. Since one can melt, they can all melt; since they can all melt, they can all melt the same night. That sorrow will come – I know it. I mean to sit up every night and look at them as long as I can keep awake; and I will impress those sparkling fields on my memory, so that, by and by, when they are taken away I can by my fancy restore those lovely myriads to the black sky and make them sparkle again, and double them by the blur of my tears.

When I look back, the Garden is a dream to me. It was beautiful, surpassingly beautiful, enchantingly beautiful; and now it is lost, and I shall not see it anymore.

The Garden is lost, but I have found *him*, and am content. He loves me as well as he can; I love him with all the strength of my passionate nature, and this, I think, is proper to my youth and sex. If I ask myself why I love him, I find I do not know, and do not really much care to know, so I suppose that this kind of love is not a product of reasoning and statistics, like one's love for other reptiles and animals. I think that this must be so. I love certain birds because of their song; but I do not love Adam on account of his singing. No, it is not that – the more he sings the more I do not get reconciled to it. Yet I ask him to sing, because I wish to learn to like everything he is interested in. I am sure I can learn, because at first I could not stand it, but now I can. It sours the milk, but it doesn't matter; I can get used to that kind of milk.

It is not on account of his brightness that I love him – no, it is not that. He is not to blame for his brightness, such as it is, for he did not make it himself; he is as God made him, and that is sufficient. There was a wise purpose in it, that I know. In time it will develop, though I think it will not be sudden; and besides, there is no hurry – he is well enough as he is.

It is not on account of his sociable and considerate ways and his delicacy that I love him. No, he has lacks in these regards, but he is well enough just so, and is improving.

It is not on account of his industry that I love him – no, it is not that. I think he has it in him, and I do not know why he conceals it from me. It is my only pain. Otherwise he is frank and open with me, now. I am sure he keeps nothing from me but this. It grieves me that he should have a secret from me, and sometimes it spoils my sleep, thinking of it, but I will put it out of my mind. It shall not trouble my happiness, which is otherwise full to overflowing.

It is not on account of his education that I love him – no, it is not that. He is self-educated, and does really know a multitude of things, but they are not so.

It is not on account of his chivalry that I love him – no, it is not that. He told on me, but I do not blame him. It is a peculiarity of sex, I think, and he did not make his sex. Of course I would not have told on him, I would have perished first; but that is a peculiarity of sex, too, and I do not take credit for it, for I did not make my sex.

Then why is it that I love him? *Merely because he is masculine*, I think.

At bottom he is good, and I love him for that, but I could love him without it. If he should beat me and abuse me, I should go on loving him. I know it, it is a matter of sex, I think.

He is strong and handsome, and I love him for that, and I admire him and am proud of him, but I could love him without those qualities. If he were plain, I should love him; if he were a wreck, I should love him; and I would work for him, and slave over him, and pray for him and watch by his bedside until I died.

Yes, I think I love him merely because he is *mine* and is *masculine*. There is no other reason, I suppose. And so I think it is as I first said: that this kind of love is not a product of reasoning and statistics. It just comes – none knows whence – and cannot explain itself. And doesn't need to.

It is what I think. But I am only a girl, and the first that examined this matter, and it may turn out that in my ignorance and inexperience I have not got it right.

It is my prayer, it is my longing, that we may pass from this life together – a longing which shall never perish from the earth, but shall have place in the heart of every wife that loves, until the end of time; and it shall be called by my name.

But if one of us must go first, it is my prayer that it shall be I; for he is strong, I am weak, I am not so necessary to him as he is to me – life without him would not be life. How could I endure it? This prayer is also immortal, and will not cease from being offered up while my race continues. I am the first wife, and in the last wife I shall be repeated.

AT EVE'S GRAVE

ADAM: Wheresoever she was, *there* was Eden.

Extract from
Eve's Autobiography

…Love, peace, comfort, measureless contentment – that was life in the Garden. It was a joy to be alive. Pain there was none, nor infirmity, nor any physical signs to mark the flight of time. Disease, care, sorrow – one might feel these outside the pale, but not in Eden. There they had no place, there they never came. All days were alike, and all a dream of delight.

Interests were abundant, for we were children, and ignorant; ignorant beyond the conception of the present day. We knew *nothing* – nothing whatever. We were starting at the very bottom of things – at the very beginning; we had to learn the ABC of things. Today the child of four years knows things which we were still ignorant of at thirty. For we were children without nurses and without instructors. There was no one to tell us anything. There was no dictionary, and we could not know whether we used our words correctly or not. We liked large ones, and I know now that we often employed them for their sound and dignity, while quite ignorant of their meaning; and as to our spelling, it was a profligate scandal. But we cared not a straw for these trifles; so that we accumulated a large and showy vocabulary, we cared nothing for the means and the methods.

But studying, learning, enquiring into the cause and nature and purpose of everything we came across, were passions with us, and this research filled our days with brilliant and absorbing interest. Adam was by constitution and proclivity a scientist; I may justly say I was the same, and we loved to call ourselves by that great name. Each was ambitious to beat the other in scientific discovery, and this incentive added a spur to our friendly rivalry, and effectively protected us against falling into idle and unprofitable ways and frivolous pleasure-seeking.

Our first memorable scientific discovery was the law that

water and like fluids run downhill, not up. It was Adam that found this out. Days and days he conducted his experiments secretly, saying nothing to me about it, for he wanted to make perfectly sure before he spoke. I knew something of prime importance was disturbing his great intellect, for his repose was troubled and he thrashed about in his sleep a good deal. But at last he was sure, and then he told me. I could not believe it, it seemed so strange, so impossible. My astonishment was his triumph, his reward. He took me from rill to rill – dozens of them – saying always, 'There – you see it runs downhill – in every case it runs downhill, never up. My theory was right; it is proven; it is established, nothing can controvert it.' And it was a pure delight to see his exultation in his great discovery.

In the present day no child wonders to see the water run down and not up, but it was an amazing thing then, and as hard to believe as any fact I have ever encountered. You see, that simple matter had been under my eyes from the day I was made, but I had never happened to notice it. It took me some time to accept it and adjust myself to it, and for a long time I could not see a running stream without voluntarily or involuntarily taking note of the dip of the surface, half expecting to see Adam's law violated. But at last I was convinced and remained so, and from that day forth I should have been startled and perplexed to see a waterfall going up the wrong way. Knowledge had to be acquired by hard work; none of it is flung at our heads gratis.

That law was Adam's first great contribution to science; and for more than two centuries it went by his name – Adam's Law of Fluidic Precipitation. Anybody could get on the soft side of him by dropping a casual compliment or two about it in his hearing. He was a good deal inflated – I will not try to conceal it – but not spoiled. Nothing ever spoiled him, he was so good and dear and right-hearted. He always put it by with such a deprecating gesture, and said it was no great thing, some other scientist would have discovered it by and by. But all the same, if a visiting stranger had audience of him and was tactless enough to forget to mention it, it was noticeable that the stranger was not invited to call again. After a couple of centuries, the discovery of the law got into dispute, and was wrangled over by scientific bodies for as much as a century, the credit being finally given to a more recent person. It was a cruel blow. Adam was never the same man afterward. He carried that sorrow in his heart for six hundred years, and I have always believed that it shortened his life. Of course throughout his days he took precedence of kings and of all the race as First Man, and had the honours due to that great rank, but these distinctions could not compensate him for that lamented ravishment, for he was a true scientist and the First; and he confided to me, more than once, that if he could have kept the glory of Discoverer of the Law of Fluidic Precipitation he would have been content to pass as his own son and Second Man. I did what I could to comfort him. I said that as First Man his fame was secure, and that a time would come when the name of the pretended discoverer of the law that water runs downhill would fade and perish and be forgotten in the earth. And I believe that. I have never ceased to believe it. That day will surely come.

I scored the next great triumph for science myself: to wit, how the milk gets into the cow. Both of us had marvelled over that mystery a long time. We had followed the cows around for years – that is, in the daytime – but had never caught them drinking a fluid of that colour. And so, at last we said they undoubtedly procured it at night. Then we took turns and watched them by night. The result was the same – the puzzle

45

remained unsolved. These proceedings were of a sort to be expected in beginners, but one perceives now that they were unscientific. A time came when experience had taught us better methods. One night as I lay musing, and looking at the stars, a grand idea flashed through my head, and I saw my way! My first impulse was to wake Adam and tell him, but I resisted and kept my secret. I slept no wink the rest of the night. The moment the first pale streak of dawn appeared I flitted stealthily away, and deep in the woods I chose a small grassy spot and wattled it in, making a secure pen; then I enclosed a cow in it. I milked her dry, then left her there, a prisoner. There was nothing there to drink – she must get milk by her secret alchemy, or stay dry.

All day I was in a fidget and could not talk connectedly I was so preoccupied, but Adam was busy trying to invent a multiplication table, and did not notice. Towards sunset he had got as far as 6 times 9 are 27, and while he was drunk with the joy of his achievement and dead to my presence and all things else, I stole away to my cow. My hand shook so with excitement and with dread of failure that for some moments I could not get a grip on a teat. Then I succeeded, and the milk came! Two gallons. Two gallons, and nothing to make it out of. I knew at once the explanation: *the milk was not taken in by the mouth, it was condensed from the atmosphere through the cow's hair*. I ran and told Adam, and his happiness was as great as mine, and his pride in me inexpressible.

Presently he said, 'Do you know, you have not made merely one weighty and far-reaching contribution to science, but two.'

And that was true. By a series of experiments we had long ago arrived at the conclusion that atmospheric air consisted of water in invisible suspension; also, that the components of water were hydrogen and oxygen in the proportion of two parts of the former to one of the latter, and expressible by the symbol H_2O. My discovery revealed the fact that there was still another ingredient – milk. We enlarged the symbol to H_2O,M.

INTERPOLATED EXTRACTS
FROM 'EVE'S DIARY'

Another discovery. One day I noticed that William McKinley was not looking well. He is the original first lion, and has been a pet of mine from the beginning. I examined him, to see what was the matter with him, and found that a cabbage which he had not chewed had stuck in his throat. I was unable to pull it out, so I took the broomstick and rammed it home. This relieved him. In the course of my labours I had made him spread his jaws, so that I could look in, and I noticed that there was something peculiar about his teeth. I now subjected them to careful and scientific examination, and the result was a consuming surprise: the lion is not a vegetarian, he is carnivorous, a flesh-eater! Intended for one, anyway.

I ran to Adam and told him, but of course he scoffed, saying, 'Where would he find flesh?'

I had to grant that I didn't know.

'Very well, then, you see yourself that the idea is apocryphal. Flesh was not intended to be eaten, or it would have been provided. No flesh having been provided, it follows, of a necessity, that no carnivora have been intruded into the scheme of things. Is this a logical deduction, or isn't it?'

'It is.'

'Is there a weak place in it anywhere?'

'No.'

'Very well, then, what have you to say?'

'That there is something better than logic.'

'Indeed? What is it?'

'Fact.'

I called a lion, and made him open his mouth.

'Look at this larboard upper jaw,' I said. 'Isn't this long forward tooth a canine?'

He was astonished, and said impressively, 'By my halidom it is!'

'What are these four, to rearward of it?'

'Premolars, or my reason totters!'

'What are these two at the back?'

'Molars, if I know a molar from a past participle when I see it. I have no more to say. Statistics cannot lie; this beast is not graminivorous.'

He is always like that – never petty, never jealous, always just, always magnanimous; prove a thing to him and he yields at once and with a noble grace. I wonder if I am worthy of this marvellous boy, this beautiful creature, this generous spirit?

It was a week ago. We examined animal after animal, then, and found the estate rich in thitherto unsuspected carnivora. Somehow it is very affecting, now, to see a stately Bengal tiger stuffing himself with strawberries and onions; it seems so out of character, though I never felt so about it before.

Later. Today, in a wood, we heard a Voice.

We hunted for it, but could not find it. Adam said he had heard it before, but had never seen it, though he had been quite close to it. So he was sure it was like the air, and could not be seen. I asked him to tell me all he knew about the Voice, but he knew very little. It was Lord of the Garden, he said, and had told him to dress the Garden and keep it; and had said we must not eat of the fruit of a certain tree and that if we ate of it we

48

should surely die. Our death would be certain. That was all he knew. I wanted to see the tree, so we had a pleasant long walk to where it stood alone in a secluded and lovely spot, and there we sat down and looked long at it with interest, and talked. Adam said it was the tree of knowledge of good and evil.

'Good and evil?'

'Yes.'

'What is that?'

'What is what?'

'Why, those things. What is good?'

'I do not know. How should I know?'

'Well, then, what is evil?'

'I suppose it is the name of something, but I do not know what.'

'But, Adam, you must have *some* idea of what it is.'

'*Why* should I have some idea? I have never seen the thing. How am I to form any conception of it? What is your own notion of it?'

Of course I had none, and it was unreasonable of me to require him to have one. There was no way for either of us to guess what it might be. It was a new word, like the other; we had not heard them before, and they meant nothing to us. My mind kept running on the matter, and presently I said, 'Adam, there are those other new words – die, and death. What do *they* mean?'

'I have no idea.'

'Well, then, what do you *think* they mean?'

'My child, cannot you see that it is impossible for me to make even a plausible *guess* concerning a matter about which I am absolutely ignorant? A person can't *think* when he has no material to think *with*. Isn't that true?'

'Yes – I know it; but how vexatious it is. Just because I can't know, I all the more *want* to know.'

We sat silent a while turning the puzzle over in our minds. Then all at once I saw how to find out, and was surprised that we had not thought of it in the beginning, it was so simple. I sprang up and said, 'How stupid we are! Let us eat of it; we shall die, and then we shall know what it is, and not have any more bother about it.'

Adam saw that it was the right idea, and he rose at once and was reaching for an apple when a most curious creature came floundering by, of a kind which we had never seen before, and of course we dropped a matter which was of no special scientific interest to rush after one that *was*.

Miles and miles over hill and dale we chased that lumbering, scrambling, fluttering goblin till we were away down the western side of the valley where the pillared great banyan tree is, and there we caught him. What a joy, what a triumph: he is a pterodactyl! Oh, he is a love, he is so ugly! And has such a temper, and such an odious cry. We called a couple of tigers and rode home, and fetched him along, and now I have him by me, and it is late, but I can't bear to go to bed, he is such a fascinating fiend and such a royal contribution to science. I know I shan't sleep for thinking of him and longing for morning to come so that I can explore him and scrutinise him, and search out the secret of his birth, and determine how much of him is bird and how much is reptile, and see if he is a survival of the fittest; which we think is doubtful, by the look of him. Oh, Science, where thou art, all other interests fade and vanish away!

Adam wakes up. Asks me not to forget to set down those four new words. It shows that he has forgotten them. But I have not. For his sake I am always watching. They are down. It is he that is building the Dictionary – as *he* thinks – but I have noticed that it is I who do the work. But it is no matter, I like to do anything that he wants me to do, and in the case of the Dictionary I take special pleasure in the labour, because it saves him a humiliation, poor boy. His spelling is unscientific. He spells cat with a *k*, and catastrophe with a *c*, although both are from the same root.

Three days later. We have named him Terry, for short, and oh, he *is* a love! All these three days we have been wholly absorbed in him. Adam wonders how science ever got along without him till now, and I feel the same. The cat took a chance in him, seeing that he was a stranger, but has regretted it. Terry fetched Thomas a rake fore and aft which left much to be desired in the way of fur, and Thomas retired with the air of a person who had been intending to confer a surprise, and was now of a mind to go and think it over and see how it happened to go the other way. Terry is just grand – there's no other creature like him. Adam has examined him thoroughly, and feels sure he is a survival of the fittest. I think Thomas thinks otherwise.

Year 3. Early in July, Adam noticed that a fish in the pond was developing legs – a fish of the whale family, though not a true whale itself, it being in a state of arrested development. It was a tadpole. We watched it with great interest, for if the legs did really mature and become usable, it was our purpose to develop them in other fishes, so that they could come out and walk around and have more liberty. We had often been troubled about those poor creatures, always wet and uncom-fortable, and always restricted to the water whilst the others were free to play amongst the flowers and have a pleasant time. Soon the legs were perfected, sure enough, and then the whale was a frog. It came ashore and hopped about and sang joyously, particularly in the evenings, and its gratitude was without bounds. Others followed rapidly, and soon we had abundant music, nights, which was a great improvement on the stillness which had prevailed before.

We brought various kinds of fishes ashore and turned them loose in the meadows, but in all cases they were a disappointment – no legs came. It was strange; we could not understand it. Within a week they had all wandered back to the water, and seemed better satisfied there than they had been on land. We took this as evidence that fishes as a rule do not care for the land, and that none of them took any strong interest in it but the whales. There were some large whales in a considerable lake three hundred miles up the valley, and Adam went up there with the idea of developing them and increasing their enjoyment.

When he had been gone a week, little Cain was born. It was a great surprise to me, I was not aware that anything was going to happen. But it is just as Adam is always saying: 'It is the unexpected that happens.'

I did not know what to make of it at first. I took it for an animal. But it hardly seemed to be that, upon examination, for it had no teeth and hardly any fur, and was a singularly helpless mite. Some of its details were human, but there were not enough of them to justify me in scientifically classifying it under that head. Thus it started as a *lusus naturae* – a freak – and it was necessary to let it go at that, for the time being, and wait for developments.

However, I soon began to take an interest in it, and this interest grew day by day; presently this interest took a warmer cast and became affection, then love, then idolatry, and all my soul went out to this creature and I was consumed with a passion of gratitude and happiness. Life was become a bliss, a rapture, an ecstasy, and I longed, day by day, hour by hour, minute by minute for Adam to return and share my unendurable joy with me.

Year 4–5. At last he came, but he did not think it was a child. He meant well, and was dear and lovely, but he was a scientist first and man afterward – it was his nature – and he could accept of nothing until it was scientifically proven. The alarms I passed through during the next twelvemonth, with that student's experiments, are quite beyond description. He exposed the child to every discomfort and inconvenience he could imagine, in order to determine what kind of bird or reptile or quadruped it was, and what it was for, and so I had to follow him about, day and night, in weariness and despair to appease its poor little sorrows and help it to bear them the best it could. He believed I had found it in the woods, and I was glad and grateful to let him think so, because the idea beguiled him to go away at times and hunt for another, and this gave the child and me blessed seasons of respite and peace. No one can ever know the relief I felt whenever he ceased from his distressful experiments and gathered his traps and bait together and started for the woods. As soon as he was out of sight I hugged my precious to my heart and smothered it with kisses, and cried for thankfulness. The poor little thing seemed to realise that something fortunate for us had happened, and it would kick and crow, and spread its gummy mouth and smile the happy smile of childhood all the way down to its brains – or whatever those things are down there.

Year 10. Next came our little Abel. I think we were a year and a half or two years old when Cain was born, and about three or three and a half when Abel was added. By this time Adam was getting to understand. Gradually his experiments grew less and less troublesome, and finally, within a year after the birth of Gladys and Edwina – years 5 and 6 – ceased altogether. He came to love the children fondly, after he had gotten them scientifically classified, and from that time till now the bliss of Eden is perfect.

We have nine children, now – half boys and half girls.

Cain and Abel are beginning to learn. Already Cain can add as well as I can, and multiply and subtract a little. Abel is not as quick as his brother, but he has persistence, and that seems to answer in the place of quickness. Abel learns about as much in three hours as Cain does, but Cain gets a couple of hours out of it for play. So, Abel is a long time on the road, but, as Adam says, he 'arrives on schedule, just the same.' Adam has concluded that persistence is one of the talents, and has classified it under that head in his Dictionary. Spelling is a gift, too, I am sure of it. With all Cain's brightness he cannot learn to spell. Now that is like his father, who is the brightest of us all, yet whose orthography is just a calamity. I can spell, and so can Abel. These several facts prove nothing, for one cannot deduce a principle from so few examples, but they do at least indicate that the ability to spell correctly is a gift; that it is born in a person, and is a sign of intellectual inferiority. By parity of reasoning, its absence is a sign of great mental power. Sometimes, when Adam has worked a good large word like 'Ratiocination' through his mill and is standing over the wreck mopping away his sweat, I could worship him he seems so intellectually grand and awful and sublime. He can spell Phthysic in more ways than there are.

Cain and Abel are dear little chaps, and they take very nice care of their little brothers and sisters. The four eldest of the flock go wandering everywhere, according to their desire, and often we see nothing of them for two or three days together. Once they lost Gladys, and came back without her. They could not remember just where or when it was they missed her. It was far away, they said, but they did not know how far; it was a new region for them. It was rich in berries of the plant which we call the *deadly nightshade* – for what reason we do not know. It hasn't any meaning, but it utilises one of the words which we long ago got of the Voice, and we like to employ new words whenever a chance offers, and so make them workable and handy. They are fond of those berries, and they long wandered about, eating them; by and by, when they were ready to go somewhere else, they missed Gladys, and she did not answer to her name.

Next day she did not come. Nor the next day, nor the day after that. Then three more days, and still she did not come. It was very strange; nothing quite the match of this had ever happened before. Our curiosity began to be excited. Adam was of the opinion that if she did not come next day, or at furthest the day after, we ought to send Cain and Abel to look.

So we did that. They were gone three days, but they found her. She had had adventures. In the dark, the first night, she fell in the river and was washed down a long distance, she did not know how far, and was finally flung upon a sandbar. After that she lived with a kangaroo's family, and was hospitably entertained, and there was much sociability. The mama-kangaroo was very sweet and motherly, and would take her babies out of her pocket and go foraging among the hills and dales and fetch home a pocketful of the choicest fruits and nuts, and nearly every night there was company – bears and rabbits and buzzards and chickens and foxes and hyenas and polecats and other creatures – and gay romping and grand times. The animals always seemed to pity the child because she had no fur, for always when she slept they covered her with leaves and moss to protect her dainty flesh, and she was covered like that when the boys found her. She had been homesick the first days, but had gotten over it.

That was her word – homesick. We have put it in the Dictionary, and will presently settle upon a meaning for it. It is made of two words which we already had, and which have clear meanings when by themselves, though apparently none when combined. Building a dictionary is exceedingly interesting work, but tough, as Adam says.

Passage from Eve's Autobiography

(Year of the World 920)

Ah, well, in that old simple, ignorant time it never entered our unthinking heads that we, humble, unknown and inconsequential little people, were cradling, nursing and watching over the most conspicuous and stupendous event which would happen in the universe for a thousand years – the founding of the human race!

It is true that the world was a solitude in the first days, but the solitude was soon modified. When we were thirty years old we had thirty children, and our children had three hundred; in twenty years more the population was six thousand; by the end of the second century it was become millions. For we are a long-lived race, and not many died. More than half of my children are still alive. I did not cease to bear until I was approaching middle age. As a rule, such of my children as survived the perils of childhood have continued to live, and this has been the case with other families. Our race now numbers billions.

EXTRACT FROM AN ARTICLE IN 'THE RADICAL',
JANUARY 916

...When the population reached five billion the earth was heavily burdened to support it. But wars, pestilences and famines brought relief, from time to time, and in some degree reduced the prodigious pressure. The memorable benefaction of the year 508, which was a famine reinforced by a pestilence, swept away sixteen hundred million people in nine months.

It was not much, but it was something. The same is all that can be said of its successors of later periods. The burden of population grew heavier and heavier and more and more formidable, century by century, and the gravity of the situation created by it was steadily and proportionately increased.

After the age of infancy, few died. The average of life was six hundred years. The cradles were filling, filling, filling – always, always, always; the cemeteries stood comparatively idle, the undertakers had but little traffic, they could hardly support their families. The death rate was 2,250 in the million. To the thoughtful this was portentous; to the light-witted it was matter for brag! These latter were always comparing the population of one decade with that of a previous one and hurrahing over the mighty increase – as if that were an advantage to the world; a world that could hardly scratch enough out of the earth to keep itself from starving.

And yet, worse was to come! Necessarily our true hope did not and could not lie in spasmodic famine and pestilence, whose effects could be only temporary, but in war and the physicians, whose help is constant. Now then, let us note what has been happening. In the past fifty years science has reduced the doctor's effectiveness by half. He uses but one deadly drug now, where formerly he used ten. Improved sanitation has made whole regions healthy which were not previously so. It has been discovered that the majority of the most useful and fatal diseases are caused by microbes of various breeds; very well, they have learned how to render the efforts of those microbes innocuous. As a result, yellow fever, black plague, cholera, diphtheria, and nearly every valuable distemper we had are become but entertainments for the idle hour, and are of no more value to the State than is the stomach-ache. Marvellous advances in surgery have been added to our disasters. They remove a diseased stomach, now, and the man gets along better and cheaper than he did before. If a man loses a faculty, they bore into his skull and restore it. They take off his legs and arms, and refurnish him from the mechanical junk shop, and he is as good as new. They give him a new nose if he needs it, new entrails, new bones, new teeth, glass eyes, silver tubes to swallow through; in a word, they take him to pieces and make him over again, and he can stand twice as much wear and tear as he could before. They do these things by help of antiseptics and anesthesia, and there is no gangrene and no pain. Thus war has become nearly valueless; out of a hundred wounded that would formerly have died, ninety-nine are back in the ranks again in a month.

What, then, is the grand result of all this microbing and sanitation and surgery? This – which is appalling: the death rate has *been reduced to 1,200 in the million*. And foolish people rejoice at it and boast about it! It is a serious matter. It promises to double the globe's population every twelve months. In time there will not be room in the world for the people to stand, let alone sit down.

Remedy? I know of none. The span of life is too long, the death rate is too trifling. The span should be thirty-five years – a mere moment of Time – the death rate should be 20,000 or 30,000 in the *million*. Even then the population would double in thirty-five years, and by and by even this would be a burden again and make the support of life difficult.

Honour to whom honour is due: the physician failed us, war has saved us. Not that the killed and wounded amount to anything as a relief, for they do not; but the poverty and desolation caused by war sweep myriads away and make space for immigrants. War is a rude friend, but a kind one. It keeps us down to sixty billion and saves the hard-grubbing world alive. It is all that the globe can support…

That Day in Eden

(Passage from Satan's Diary)

Long ago I was in the bushes near the Tree of Knowledge when the Man and Woman came there and had a conversation. I was present, now, when they came again after all these years. They were as before – mere boy and girl – trim, rounded, slender, flexible, snow images lightly flushed with the pink of the skies, innocently unconscious of their nakedness, lovely to look upon, beautiful beyond words.

I listened again. Again as in that former time they puzzled over those words, 'good', 'evil', 'death', and tried to reason out their meaning; but, of course, they were not able to do it. Adam said, 'Come, maybe we can find Satan. He might know these things.'

Then I came forth, still gazing upon Eve and admiring, and said to her, 'You have not seen me before, sweet creature, but I have seen you. I have seen all the animals, but in beauty none of them equals you. Your hair, your eyes, your face, your flesh tints, your form, the tapering grace of your white limbs – all are beautiful, adorable, perfect.'

It gave her pleasure, and she looked herself over, putting out a foot and a hand and admiring them; then she naively said, 'It is a joy to be so beautiful. And Adam – he is the same.'

She turned him about, this way and that, to show him off, with such guileless pride in her blue eyes, and he – he took it all as just matter of course, and was innocently happy in it, and said, 'When I have flowers on my head, it is better still.'

Eve said, 'It is true – you shall see,' and she flitted hither and thither like a butterfly and plucked flowers, and in a moment laced their stems together in a glowing wreath and set it upon his head; then tiptoed and gave it a pat here and there with her nimble fingers, with each pat enhancing its grace and shape; none knows how, nor why it should so result, but in it there is a law somewhere, though the delicate art and mystery of it is her secret alone, and not learnable by another; and when at last it was to her mind, she clapped her hands for pleasure, then reached up and kissed him – as pretty a sight, taken altogether, as in my experience I have seen.

Presently, to the matter in hand. The meaning of those words – would I tell her?

Certainly none could be more willing, but how was I to do it? I could think of no way to make her understand, and I said so. I said, 'I will try, but it is hardly of use. For instance – what is pain?'

'Pain? I do not know.'

'Certainly. How should you? Pain is not of your world; pain is impossible to you; you have never experienced a physical pain. Reduce that to a formula, a principle, and what have we?'

'What have we?'

'This: things which are outside of our orbit – our own particular world – things which by our constitution and equipment we are unable to see, or feel, or otherwise experience – *cannot be made comprehensible to us in words.* There you have the whole thing in a nutshell. It is a principle, it is axiomatic, it is a law. Now do you understand?'

The gentle creature looked dazed, and for all result she was delivered of this vacant remark: 'What is axiomatic?'

She had missed the point. Necessarily she would. Yet her effort was success for me, for it was a vivid confirmation of the truth of what I have been saying. Axiomatic was for the present a thing outside of the world of her experience, therefore it has no meaning for her. I ignored her question and continued: 'What is fear?'

'Fear? I do not know.'

'Naturally. Why should you? You have not felt it, you cannot feel it, it does not belong in your world. With a hundred thousand words I should not be able to make you understand what fear is. How then am I to explain it to you? You have never seen it, it is foreign to your world, it is impossible to make that word mean anything to you, so far as I can see. In a way, it is a sleep –'

'Oh, I know what that is!'

'But it is a sleep only in a way, as I said. It is more than a sleep.'

'Sleep is pleasant, sleep is lovely!'

'But death is a long sleep – very long.'

'Oh, all the lovelier! Therefore I think nothing could be better than death.'

I said to myself, 'Poor child, some day you may know what a pathetic truth you have spoken; some day you may say, out of a broken heart, "Come to me, O Death the compassionate! Steep me in the merciful oblivion, O refuge of the sorrowful, friend of the forsaken and the desolate!"' Then I said aloud, 'But this sleep is eternal.'

The word went over her head. Necessarily it would.

'Eternal. What is eternal?'

'Ah, that also is outside of your world, as yet. There is no way to make you understand it.'

It was a hopeless case. Words referring to things outside of her experience were a foreign language to her, and meaningless. She was like a little baby whose mother says to it, 'Don't put your finger in the candle flame; it will burn you.' Burn – it is a foreign word to the baby, and will have no terrors for it until experience shall have revealed its meaning. It is not worthwhile for mamma to make the remark, the baby will googoo cheerfully, and put its finger in the pretty flame – once. After these private reflections I said again that I did not think there was any way to make her understand the meaning of the word eternal.

She was silent awhile, turning these deep matters over in the unworn machinery of her mind; then she gave up the puzzle and shifted her ground, saying, 'Well, there are those other words. What is good, and what is evil?'

'It is another difficulty. They, again, are outside of your world; they have place in the moral kingdom only. You have no morals.'

'What are morals?'

'A system of law which distinguishes between right and wrong, good morals and bad. These things do not exist for you. I cannot make it clear; you would not understand.'

'But try.'

'Well, obedience to constituted authority is a moral law. Suppose Adam should forbid you to put your child in the river and leave it there overnight – would you put the child there?'

She answered with a darling simplicity and guilelessness: 'Why, yes, if I wanted to?'

'There, it is just as I said – you would not know any better; you have no idea of duty, command, obedience; they have no meaning for you. In your present state you are in no possible way responsible for anything you do or say or think. It is impossible for you to do wrong, for you have no more notion of right and wrong than the other animals have. You and they can do only right; whatever you and they do is right and innocent. It is a divine estate, the loftiest and purest attainable in heaven and in earth. It is the angel gift. The angels are wholly pure and sinless, for they do not know right from wrong, and all the acts of such are blameless. No one can do wrong without knowing how to distinguish between right and wrong.'

'Is it an advantage to know?'

'Most certainly not! That knowledge would remove all that is divine, all that is angelic, from the angels, and immeasurably degrade them.'

'Are there any persons that know right from wrong?'

'Not in – well, not in heaven.'

'What gives that knowledge?'

'The Moral Sense.'

'What is that?'

'Well – no matter. Be thankful that you lack it.'

'Why?'

'Because it is a degradation, a disaster. Without it one cannot do wrong; with it, one can. Therefore it had but one office, only one – to teach how to do wrong. It can teach no other thing – no other thing whatever. It is the *creator* of wrong; wrong cannot exist until the Moral Sense brings it into being.'

'How can one acquire the Moral Sense?'

'By eating of the fruit of the Tree, here. But why do you wish to know? Would you like to have the Moral Sense?'

She turned wistfully to Adam: 'Would you like to have it?'

He showed no particular interest, and only said, 'I am indifferent. I have not understood any of this talk, but if you like we will eat it, for I cannot see that there is any objection to it.'

Poor ignorant things, the command of refrain had meant nothing to them, they were but children, and could not understand untried things and verbal abstractions which stood for matters outside of their little world and their narrow experience. Eve reached for an apple! – oh, farewell, Eden and your sinless joys! Come poverty and pain, hunger and cold and heartbreak, bereavement, tears and shame, envy, strife, malice and dishonour, age, weariness, remorse; then desperation and the prayer for the release of death, indifferent that the gates of hell yawn beyond it!

She tasted – the fruit fell from her hand.

It was pitiful. She was like one who wakens slow and confusedly out of a sleep. She gazed half vacantly at me, then at Adam, holding her curtaining fleece of golden hair back with her hand; then her wandering glance fell upon her naked person. The red blood mounted to her cheek, and she sprang behind a bush and stood there crying, and saying, 'Oh, my modesty is lost to me – my unoffending form is become a shame to me!' She moaned and muttered in her pain, and dropped her head, saying, 'I am degraded – I have fallen, oh, so low, and I shall never rise again.'

Adam's eyes were fixed upon her in a dreamy amazement, for he could not understand what had happened, it being outside his world as yet, and her words having no meaning for one void of the Moral Sense. And how his wonder grew! For, unknown to Eve, her hundred years rose upon her, and faded the heaven of her eyes and the tints of her young flesh, and touched her hair with grey, and traced faint sprays of wrinkles about her mouth and eyes, and shrunk her form, and dulled the satin lustre of her skin.

All this the fair boy saw: then loyally and bravely he took the apple and tasted it, saying nothing.

The change came upon him also. Then he gathered boughs for both and clothed their nakedness, and they turned and went their way, hand in hand and bent with age, and so passed from sight.

Eve Speaks

I

They drove us from the Garden with their swords of flame, the fierce cherubim. And what had we done? We meant no harm. We were ignorant and did as any other children might do. We could not know it was wrong to disobey the command, for the words were strange to us and we did not understand them. We did not know right from wrong – how should we know? We could not, without the Moral Sense; it was not possible. If we had been given the Moral Sense first – ah, that would have been fairer, that would have been kinder; then we should be to blame if we disobeyed. But to say to us poor ignorant children words which we could not understand, and then punish us because we did not do as we were told – ah, how can that be justified? We knew no more then than this littlest child of mine knows now, with its four years – oh, not so much, I think. Would I say to it, 'If thou touchest this bread I will overwhelm thee with unimaginable disaster, even to the dissolution of thy corporeal elements,' and when it took the bread and smiled up in my face, thinking no harm, as not understanding those strange words, would I take advantage of its innocence and strike it down with the mother hand it trusted? Whoso knoweth the mother heart, let him judge if it would do that thing. Adam says my brain is turned by my troubles and that I am become wicked. I am as I am; I did not make myself.

They drove us out. Drove us out into this harsh wilderness, and shut the gates against us. We that had meant no harm. It is three months. We were ignorant then; we are rich in learning, now – ah, how rich! We know hunger, thirst, and cold; we know pain, disease, and grief; we know hate, rebellion, and deceit; we know remorse, the conscience that prosecutes guilt and innocence alike, making no distinction; we know weariness of body and spirit, the unrefreshing sleep, the rest which rests not, the dreams which restore Eden, and banish it again with the waking; we know misery; we know torture and the heartbreak; we know humiliation and insult; we know indecency, immodesty, and the soiled mind; we know the scorn that attaches to the transmitted image of God exposed unclothed to the day; we know fear; we know vanity, folly, envy, hypocrisy; we know irreverence; we know blasphemy; we know right from wrong, and how to avoid the one and do the other; we know all the rich product of the Moral Sense, and it is our possession. Would we could sell it for one hour of Eden and white purity; would we could degrade the animals with it!

We have it all – that treasure. All but death. Death… death. What may that be?

Adam comes.

'Well?'

'He still sleeps.'

That is our second-born – our Abel.

'He has slept enough for his good, and his garden suffers for his care. Wake him.'

'I have tried and cannot.'

'Then he is very tired. Let him sleep on.'

'I think it is his hurt that makes him sleep so long.'

I answer: 'It may be so. Then we will let him rest; no doubt the sleep is healing it.'

II

It is a day and a night, now, that he has slept. We found him by his altar in his field, that morning, his face and body drenched in blood. He said his eldest brother struck him down. Then he spoke no more and fell asleep. We laid him in his bed and washed the blood away, and were glad to know the hurt was light and that he had no pain; for if he had pain he would not have slept.

It was in the early morning that we found him. All day he slept that sweet, reposeful sleep, lying always on his back, and never moving, never turning. It showed how tired he was, poor thing. He is so good and works so hard, rising with the dawn and labouring till the dark. And now he is overworked; it will be best that he tax himself less, after this, and I will ask him; he will do anything I wish.

All the day he slept. I know, for I was always near, and made dishes for him and kept them warm against his waking. Often I crept in and fed my eyes upon his gentle face, and was thankful for that blessed sleep. And still he slept on – slept with his eyes wide; a strange thing, and made me think he was awake at first, but it was not so, for I spoke and he did not answer. He always answers when I speak. Cain had moods and will not answer, but not Abel.

I have sat by him all the night, being afraid he might wake and want his food. His face was very white; and it changed, and he came to look as he had looked when he was a little child in Eden long ago, so sweet and good and dear. It carried me back over the abyss of years, and I was lost in dreams and tears – oh, hours, I think. Then I came to myself; and thinking he stirred, I kissed his cheek to wake him, but he slumbered on and I was disappointed. His cheek was cold, I brought sacks of wool and the down of birds and covered him, but he was still cold, and I brought more. Adam has come again, and says he is not yet warm. I do not understand it.

III

We cannot wake him! With my arms clinging about him I have looked into his eyes, through the veil of my tears, and begged for one little word, and he will not answer. Oh, is it that long sleep – is it death? And will he wake no more?

FROM SATAN'S DIARY

Death has entered the world, the creatures are perishing; one of The Family is fallen; the product of the Moral Sense is complete. The Family think ill of death – they will change their minds.

Adam's Soliloquy

*The spirit of Adam is supposed to be visiting New York City
inspecting the dinosaur at the Museum of Natural History.*

It is strange... very strange. *I* do not remember this creature.
(*After gazing long and admiringly.*) Well, it is wonderful! The
mere *skeleton* fifty-seven feet long and sixteen feet high! Thus
far, it seems, they've found only this sample – without doubt a
merely medium-sized one. A person could not step out here
into the Park and happen by luck upon the largest horse in
America; no, he would happen upon one that would look
small alongside of the biggest Normandy. It is quite likely that
the biggest dinosaur was ninety feet long and twenty feet high.
It would be five times as long as an elephant; an elephant
would be to it what a calf is to an elephant. The bulk of the
creature! The weight of him! As long as the longest whale, and
twice the substance in him! And all good wholesome pork,
most likely; meat enough to last a village a year... Think of a
hundred of them in line, draped in shining cloth of gold! – a
majestic thing for a coronation procession. But expensive, for
he would eat much; only kings and millionaires could afford
him.

I have no recollection of him; neither Eve nor I had heard
about him until yesterday. We spoke to Noah about him; he
coloured and changed the subject. Being brought back to it –
and pressed a little – he confessed that in the matter of stock-
ing the Ark the stipulations had not been carried out with
absolute strictness – that is, in minor details, unessentials.
There were some irregularities. He said the boys were to
blame for this – the boys mainly, his own fatherly indulgence
partly. They were in the giddy heyday of their youth at the
time, the happy springtime of life; their hundred years sat
upon them lightly, and – well, he had once been a boy himself,

and he had not the heart to be too exacting with them. And so – well, they did things they shouldn't have done, and he – to be candid, he winked. But on the whole they did pretty faithful work, considering their age. They collected and stowed a good share of the really useful animals; and also, when Noah was not watching, a multitude of useless ones, such as flies, mosquitoes, snakes, and so on, but they did certainly leave ashore a good many creatures which might possibly have had value some time or other, in the course of time. Mainly these were vast saurians a hundred feet long, and monstrous mammals, such as the megatherium and that sort, and there was really some excuse for leaving them behind, for two reasons: (1) it was manifest that some time or other they would be needed as fossils for museums and (2) there had been a miscalculation – the Ark was smaller than it should have been, and so there wasn't room for those creatures. There was actually fossil material enough all by itself to freight twenty-five Arks like that one. As for the dinosaur… But Noah's conscience was easy; it was not named in his cargo list and he and the boys were not aware that there was such a creature. He said he could not blame himself for not knowing about the dinosaur because it was an American animal, and America had not then been discovered.

Noah went on to say, 'I did reproach the boys for not making the most of the room we had, by discarding trashy animals and substituting beasts like the mastodon, which could be useful to man in doing heavy work such as the elephant performs, but they said those great creatures would have increased our labours beyond our strength, in the matter of feeding and watering them, we being short-handed. There was something in that. We had no pump; there was but one window; we had to let down a bucket from that, and haul it up a good fifty feet, which was very tiresome; then we had to carry the water downstairs – fifty feet again, in cases where it was for the elephants and their kind, for we kept them in the hold to serve for ballast. As it was, we lost many animals – choice animals that would have been valuable in menageries – different breeds of lions, tigers, hyenas, wolves, and so on; for they wouldn't drink the water after the sea salt water got mixed with the fresh. But we never lost a locust, nor a grasshopper, nor a weevil, nor a rat, nor a cholera germ, nor any of that sort of beings. On the whole, I think we did very well, everything considered. We were shepherds and farmers; we had never been to sea before; we were ignorant of naval matters, and I know this for certain, that there is more difference between agriculture and navigation than a person would think. It is my opinion that the two trades do not belong together. Shem thinks the same; so does Japeth. As for what Ham thinks, it is not important. Ham is biased. You find me a Presbyterian that isn't, if you think you can.'

He said it aggressively; it had in it the spirit of a challenge. I avoided argument by changing the subject. With Noah, arguing is a passion, a disease, and it is growing upon him; had been growing upon him for thirty thousand years, and more. It makes him unpopular, unpleasant; many of his oldest friends dread to meet him. Even strangers soon get to avoiding him, although at first they are glad to meet him and gaze at him, on account of his celebrated adventure. For a time they are proud of his notice because he is so distinguished, but he argues them to rags, and before long they begin to wish, like the rest, that something had happened to the Ark.

On the bench in the Park, mid afternoon, dreamily noting
the drift of the human species back and forth.

To think – this multitude is but a wee little fraction of the earth's population! And all blood kin to me, every one! Eve ought to have come with me; this would excite her affectionate heart. She was never able to keep her composure when she came upon a relative; she would try to kiss every one of these people, black and white and all. (*A baby wagon passes.*) How little change one can notice – none at all, in fact. I remember the first child well. Let me see… it is three hundred thousand years ago come Tuesday. This one is just like it. So between the first one and the last one there is really nothing to choose. The same insufficiency of hair, the same absence of teeth, the same feebleness of body and apparent vacancy of mind, the same general unattractiveness all around. Yet Eve worshipped that early one, and it was pretty to see her with it. This latest one's mother worships *it*; it shows in her eyes – it is the very look that used to shine in Eve's. To think that so subtle and intangible a thing as a *look* could flit and flash from face to face down a procession three hundred thousand years long and remain the same, without shade of change! Yet here it is, lighting this young creature's face just as it lighted Eve's long ago – the newest thing I have seen in the earth, and the oldest. Of course, the dinosaur… But that is another class.

She drew the baby wagon to the bench and sat down and began to shove it softly back and forth with one hand while she held up a newspaper with the other and absorbed herself in its contents. Presently: 'My!' she exclaimed; which startled me, and I ventured to ask her, modestly and respectfully, what was the matter. She courteously passed the paper to me and said, pointing with her finger, 'There – it reads like fact, but I don't know.'

It was very embarrassing. I tried to look at my ease, and nonchalantly turned the paper this and that and the other way, but her eye was upon me and I felt that I was not succeeding. Pretty soon she asked, hesitatingly, 'Can't – can't – you – read?'

I had to confess that I couldn't. It filled her with wonder. But it had one pleasant effect – it interested her in me, and I was thankful, for I was getting lonesome for someone to talk to and listen to. The young fellow who was showing me around – on his own motion, I did not invite him – had missed his appointment at the Museum, and I was feeling disappointed, for he was good company. When I told the young woman I could not read, she asked me another embarrassing question:

'Where are you from?'

I skirmished – to gain time and position. I said, 'Make a guess. See how near you come.'

She brightened and exclaimed, 'I shall dearly like it, sir, if you don't mind. If I guess right will you tell me?'

'Yes.'

'Honour bright?'

'Honour bright? What is that?'

She laughed delightedly and said, 'That's a good start! I was *sure* that that phrase would catch you. I know one thing, now, all right. I know –'

'What do you know?'

'That you are not an American. And you aren't, *are* you?'

'No. You are right. I'm not – honour bright, as you say.'

She looked immensely pleased with herself, and said, 'I reckon I'm not always smart, but *that* was smart, anyway. But not so *very*, after all, because I already knew – believed I knew

– that you were a foreigner, by another sign.'

'What was that?'

'Your accent.'

She was an accurate observer. I do speak English with a heavenly accent, and she had detected a foreign twang in it. She ran charmingly on, most naively and engagingly pleased with her triumph: 'The minute you said, "See 'ow near you come to it," I said to myself, "Two to one he is a foreigner, and ten to one he's English." Now that *is* your nationality, *isn't* it?'

I was sorry to spoil her victory, but I had to do it: 'Ah – you'll have to guess again.'

'What – you are not an Englishman?'

'No – honour bright.'

She looked me searchingly over, evidently communing with herself – adding up my points, then she said: 'Well, you don't *look* like an Englishman, and that is true.' After a little she added, 'The fact is you don't look like *any* foreigner – not quite like… like *anybody* I've seen before. I will guess some more.'

She guessed every country whose name she could think of and grew gradually discouraged. Finally she said, 'You must be the Man Without a Country – the one the story tells about. You don't seem to have any nationality at all. How did you come to come to America? Have you any kinfolks here?'

'Yes – several.'

'Oh, then you came to see *them*.'

'Partly – yes.'

She sat awhile, thinking, then: 'Well, I'm not going to give up quite yet. Where do you live when you are at home – in a city, or in the country?'

'Which do you think?'

'Well, I don't quite know. You *do* look a little countrified, if

84

you don't mind my saying it, but you look a little citified, too – not much, but a little, although you can't read, which is very curious, and you are not used to newspapers. Now *my* guess is that you live mainly in the country when you are at home, and not very much in the city. Is that right?'

'Yes, quite right.'

'Oh, good! Now I'll take a fresh start.'

Then she wore herself to the bone naming cities. No success. Next she wanted me to help her a little with some 'pointers', as she phrased it. Was my city large? Yes. Was it very large? Yes. Did they have mobiles there? No. Electric light? No. Railroads, hospitals, colleges, cops? No.

'Why, then, it is not civilised! Where *can* that place be? Be good and tell me just one peculiarity of it – then maybe I can guess.'

'Well, then, just one; it has gates of pearl.'

'Oh, go along! That's the New Jerusalem. It isn't fair to joke. Never mind. I'll guess it yet – it will come into my head pretty soon, just when I'm not expecting it. Oh, I've got an idea! Please talk a little in your own language – that'll be a good pointer.' I accommodated her with a sentence or two. She shook her head despondently.

'No,' she said, 'it doesn't sound human. I mean, it doesn't sound like any of those other foreigners. It's pretty enough – it's quite pretty, I think – but I'm sure I've not heard it before. Maybe if you were to pronounce your name… What *is* your name, if you'll be so good?'

'Adam.'

'Adam?'

'Yes.'

'But Adam *what*?'

'That is all – just Adam.'

'Nothing at all but just that? Why, how curious! There's plenty of Adams; how can they tell you from the rest?'

'Oh, that is no trouble. I'm the only one there is, there where I'm from.'

'Upon my word! Well, it beats the band! It reminds a person of the old original. That was his name, too, and he hadn't any but that – just like you.' Then, archly, 'You've heard of him, I suppose?'

'Oh, yes! Do you know him? Have you ever seen him?'

'*Seen* him? Seen *Adam*? Thanks to goodness, no! It would scare me into fits.'

'I don't see why.'

'You don't?'

'No.'

'*Why* don't you see why?'

'Because there is no sense in a person being scared of his kin.'

'*Kin*?'

'Yes. Isn't he a distant relative of yours?'

She thought it was prodigiously funny, and said it was perfectly true, but *she* never would have been bright enough to think it. I found it a new and most pleasant sensation to have my wit admired, and was about to try to do some more when that young fellow came. He planted himself on the other side of the young woman and began a vapid remark about the weather, but she gave him a look that withered him and got stiffly up and wheeled the baby away.

A Monument to Adam

Someone has revealed to the *Tribune* that I once suggested to Rev. Thomas K. Beecher, of Elmira, New York, that we get up a monument to Adam, and that Mr Beecher favoured the project. There is more to it than that. The matter started as a joke, but it came somewhat near to materialising.

It is long ago – thirty years. Mr Darwin's *Descent of Man* had been in print five or six years, and the storm of indignation raised by it was still raging in pulpits and periodicals. In tracing the genesis of the human race back to its sources, Mr Darwin had left Adam out altogether. We had monkeys, and 'missing links', and plenty of other kinds of ancestors, but no Adam. Jesting with Mr Beecher and other friends in Elmira, I said there seems to be a likelihood that the world would discard Adam and accept the monkey, and that in the course of time Adam's very name would be forgotten in the earth. Therefore this calamity ought to be averted – a monument would accomplish this, and Elmira ought not to waste this honourable opportunity to do Adam a favour and herself a credit.

Then the unexpected happened. Two bankers came forward and took hold of the matter – not for fun, not for sentiment, but because they saw in the monument certain commercial advantages for the town. The projects had seemed gently humorous before – it was more than that now, with this stern business gravity injected into it. The bankers discussed the monument with me. We met several times. They proposed an indestructible memorial, to cost twenty-five thousand dollars. The insane oddity of a monument in a village to preserve a name that would outlast the hills and the rocks without any such help would advertise Elmira to the ends of the earth – and draw custom. It would be the only monument on the planet to Adam, and in the matter of interest and impressiveness could never have a rival until somebody should set up a monument to the Milky Way.

People would come from every corner of the globe and stop off to look at it, no tour of the world would be complete that left out Adam's monument. Elmira would be a Mecca; there would be pilgrim ships at pilgrim rates, pilgrim specials on the continent's railways; libraries would be written about the monument, every tourist would Kodak it, models of it would be for sale everywhere in the earth, its form would become as familiar as the figure of Napoleon.

One of the bankers subscribed five thousand dollars, and I think the other one subscribed half as much, but I do not remember with certainty now whether that was the figure or not. We got designs made – some of them came from Paris.

In the beginning – as a detail of the project when it was as yet a joke – I had framed a humble and beseeching and per-fervid petition to Congress begging the government to build the monument, as a testimony to the Great Republic's grati-tude to the Father of the Human Race and as a token of her loyalty to him in this dark day of his humiliation when his older children were doubting him and deserting him. It seemed to me that this petition ought to be presented, now – it would be widely and feelingly abused and ridiculed and cursed, and would advertise our scheme and make our groundfloor stock go off briskly. So I sent it to General Joseph R. Hawley, who was then in the House, and he said he would present it. But he did not do it. I think he explained that when he came to read it he was afraid of it: it was too serious, too gushy, too sentimental – the House might take it for earnest.

We ought to have carried out our monument scheme; we could have managed it without any great difficulty, and Elmira would now be the most celebrated town in the universe.

Very recently I began to build a book in which one of the minor characters touches incidentally upon a project for a monument to Adam, and now the *Tribune* has come upon a trace of the forgotten jest of thirty years ago. Apparently mental telegraphy is still in business. It is odd; but the freaks of mental telegraphy are usually odd.

NOTE ON THE TEXT

The text of 'The Diary of Adam and Eve' in the version it appears here was first published as 'Eve's Diary' and 'Extracts from Adam's Diary' in *The $30,000 Bequest and Other Stories*, 1906; 'Extract from Eve's Autobiography' and 'Passage from Eve's Autobiography' were first published in *Letters from the Earth* by Mark Twain, edited by Bernard DeVoto, 1962 (reproduced here by kind permission of HarperCollins Inc.); 'That Day in Eden', 'Eve Speaks' and 'Adam's Soliloquy' first appeared in *Europe and Elsewhere*, 1923; and 'A Monument to Adam' was first published in *The $30,000 Bequest and Other Stories*, 1906.

BIOGRAPHICAL NOTE

Mark Twain was born Samuel Langhorne Clemens in 1835 in Florida. Soon after his birth his family moved to Hannibal, Missouri, where he spent his childhood. Following his father's death in 1847, Twain worked as a printer for a newspaper owned by his brother, before finding employment in New York and Philadelphia, again as a printer. From 1857 to 1861, he worked as a river pilot on the Mississippi, before moving firstly to Virginia City, and then to California to take up a position as a newspaper correspondent. A successful short story in 1865 quickly inspired a collection entitled *The Celebrated Jumping Frog of Calaveras County, and Other Sketches* (1867), and further volumes swiftly followed. With striking effect, Twain prioritised the method of telling a story over its outcome, and, though a prolific writer of satires, travelogues, essays, and letters, he is best remembered for his picaresque depictions of Missouri life: namely his 1876 novel, *The Adventures of Tom Sawyer*, and its sequel, *The Adventures of Huckleberry Finn* (1884).

In 1870 Twain married Olivia Langdon. Her death in 1904, together with the loss of their daughter, Susan, and the onset of financial difficulties in the 1890s, had an impact on Twain's later work; potboilers were written for money, and other works became darker in tone. Twain spent much of the 1890s in Europe, residing by turns in England, Switzerland, Austria and France, before returning to New York in 1900 and then settling in Connecticut. He died on 21 April 1910.

HESPERUS PRESS

Hesperus Press is committed to bringing near what is far – far both in space and time. Works written by the greatest authors, and unjustly neglected or simply little known in the English-speaking world, are made accessible through new translations and a completely fresh editorial approach. Through these classic works, the reader is introduced to the greatest writers from all times and all cultures.

For more information on Hesperus Press, please visit our website: **www.hesperuspress.com**

FULL LIST OF TITLES IN THE HESPERUS ANNIVERSARY REPRINTS SERIES